Written by
Robin Mitchell

Princess Pumpalot
(The Farting Princess)

Illustrated by Katherine Jones

The Cadies & Witchery Tours Publishing

First published in 2012

The Cadies & Witchery Tours Publishing
84 West Bow (Victoria Street)
Edinburgh
Scotland
EH1 2HH

t: +44 (0) 131 225 6745
e: info@witcherytours.com
w: www.witcherytours.com

ISBN 978-0-9522927-5-3

Designed and printed by Juicy Design
t: +44 (0) 1777 711 313
w: www.juicydesign.co.uk

A big thank you to:

Robin Bankhead

Aidan Baxter

Emily Baxter

Keith Bradley

Rebecca Bricker

Alexander Clapperton

Yasmin Fedda

Jim Hickey

Adam Lyal

Gordon McCulloch

Euan MacInnes

Alison Mitchell

Brian Mitchell

May Mitchell

Cameron Pirie

Anna Spiga

Derek Stores

Mrs Woo

INT. LORD DIPPY HUGHES'S LIBRARY - DAY

LORD DIPPY HUGHES is sitting in a comfy armchair, with a large dusty book open in front of him. He is dressed as a clown.

He reads from the book.

> LORD DIPPY HUGHES
> Princess Pumpalot lives with her parents, the King and the Queen, in a large castle on top of a rocky hill. The only way in and out of the castle is by a long, narrow tunnel, which runs under a lake and connects the castle with the village of Wiffyville.

LORD DIPPY HUGHES looks up.

> LORD DIPPY HUGHES (CONT'D)
> The layout of the village was designed by me. I'm a clown-turned-architect. I arranged the buildings in the shape of a smiley face.

LORD DIPPY HUGHES turns a page in the book.

> LORD DIPPY HUGHES (CONT'D)
> At the centre of the village is a large, gothic tower. This is where two princes stay. They are twins, Prince Nastavia and Prince Niceavia.

LORD DIPPY HUGHES closes the book.

                    LORD DIPPY HUGHES (CONT'D)
          Before we get underway, can I just say that
          this story has been written in the style of a
          screenplay. It is how a story is written on the
          page before it appears in the cinema.

LORD DIPPY HUGHES pours himself a glass of milk.

                    LORD DIPPY HUGHES (CONT'D)
          The scene headings are shown by INT which
          means interior and EXT which means exterior.
          There are brief descriptions of the action, and
          the dialogue appears under each character's
          name. When we move from one scene to
          another, you will see the transition, CUT TO.
          I'm sure you'll work everything else out for
          yourself. It's easy to follow.

LORD DIPPY HUGHES takes a drink from his glass
of milk.

                    LORD DIPPY HUGHES (CONT'D)
          If you want some good advice, it's lots of fun
          making up voices for each of the characters and
          reading the dialogue out loud. Happy reading.

                                                    CUT TO:

INT. KING'S CHAMBERS - DAY

The KING sits at a table eating cheese and biscuits.

8

SIDNEY the servant, holding a long spear, stands in the corner of the room.

The QUEEN is sitting on her throne. She is talking on her mobile phone.

> QUEEN
>
> Can you find Princess Pumpalot and send her up to see us?
> (pause)
> I don't care if she's just finished her game of rugby, send her up now!

The QUEEN switches off her mobile phone and throws it on the table. She turns to the KING.

> QUEEN (CONT'D)
>
> You just can't get the servants these days. The last advert I put up in the job centre only attracted three candidates, and one of them was a giraffe.

> KING
>
> Geoffrey is a nice giraffe. Polite and mild-mannered.

> QUEEN
>
> Yes, he is polite and mild-mannered, but he's hopeless at carrying trays.

KING

Well, I'm sure if you were a long-necked, hoofed mammal, you'd be hopeless at carrying trays too.

QUEEN

I can't believe you insisted that we kept him on.

KING

Him! His name is Geoffrey and he's an excellent lookout.

QUEEN

We weren't looking for a lookout. And as for Loots and Sidney . . .

Their discussion is interrupted by a mouse running across the floor.

The QUEEN screams and jumps on her throne.

QUEEN (CONT'D)

Not another mouse! That's the fourth one this week! You'll have to stop eating cheese and biscuits.

KING

Oh, but you know how much I love my Stilton.

There is a loud knock on the door.

The KING points to a book on the table.

KING (CONT'D)

You better hide that.

The QUEEN picks up the book. We see the back cover. It shows the face of a BEARDED WITCH. The QUEEN hides the book behind a cushion on her throne.

SIDNEY the servant approaches the door. As he attempts to open it, he drops his spear. The QUEEN shakes her head.

SIDNEY the servant opens the door to reveal a pair of giraffe legs on the other side of the door.

A small hatch in the ceiling opens. GEOFFREY the giraffe sticks his head through the hatch. He bows his head towards the KING and the QUEEN.

GEOFFREY

Your Majesties, Princess Pumpalot is here to see you.

PRINCESS PUMPALOT walks into the room. She is wearing a long dress and a pair of rugby boots. Her dress and face are covered in mud. She has a rugby ball under her right arm.

The QUEEN rolls her eyes.

QUEEN

Look at the state of you. It's not very ladylike.

PRINCESS PUMPALOT

What constitutes ladylike?

12

QUEEN
Not playing rugby for a start.

PRINCESS PUMPALOT
Just because I don't like shoes doesn't make me less of a Princess.

QUEEN
If you insist on playing rugby, could you wear something other than your dress?

PRINCESS PUMPALOT
Would you prefer I wore an evening gown?

QUEEN
That's a stupid thing to say.

The KING interrupts.

KING
Now, now. Stop this. We have important matters to discuss.

PRINCESS PUMPALOT
She started it.

QUEEN
No, I didn't.

KING
I said stop this!

13

The QUEEN turns her head away. The KING looks over to PRINCESS PUMPALOT.

                    KING (CONT'D)
          Did you win your game against Wiffyville
          Under-Thirteens?

The QUEEN looks over to the KING.

                      QUEEN
          You just encourage her.

                       KING
          Just showing some interest in our daughter.

              PRINCESS PUMPALOT
          We won 26-3. Guffy scored the winning try.

                      QUEEN
          Oh! It gets worse.

PRINCESS PUMPALOT turns to the QUEEN.

              PRINCESS PUMPALOT
          What's wrong now?

                      QUEEN
          Guffy shouldn't be playing in the Royal Team.

              PRINCESS PUMPALOT
          Guffy is our best player.

                      QUEEN
          Guffy is a servant.

                    PRINCESS PUMPALOT
            He's no different from you and me.

                        QUEEN
            Don't be ridiculous.

The KING steps between the QUEEN and PRINCESS
PUMPALOT.

                        KING
            Right, let's call a halt to this now. I've had
            enough of this bickering.

PRINCESS PUMPALOT looks up at the ceiling.

The QUEEN folds her arms.

                                            CUT TO:

EXT. TOP OF GOTHIC TOWER, WIFFYVILLE - DAY

Twin brothers PRINCE NASTAVIA and PRINCE
NICEAVIA are on their roof garden. PRINCE NASTAVIA
is placing a telescope between two small bushes.

                    PRINCE NICEAVIA
            What have you been spending your money
            on now?

                    PRINCE NASTAVIA
            A telescope.

15

PRINCE NICEAVIA
Where did you get this from?

PRINCE NASTAVIA
Can you not read?

PRINCE NASTAVIA points to the base of the telescope. It has the inscription, VILLAGE OBSERVATORY.

PRINCE NASTAVIA (CONT'D)
The Village Observatory was selling off their old telescope.

PRINCE NICEAVIA
I didn't know you were interested in the night sky?

PRINCE NASTAVIA
I'm not. It's to keep an eye on the tenants renting my bungalows in the village.

PRINCE NICEAVIA
(disbelief)
You're 13 years old and renting bungalows!

PRINCE NASTAVIA
Better than doing a paper round. The bungalows give me a good return on my investment.

PRINCE NICEAVIA
I can't believe you knocked down perfectly good cottages and replaced them with modern bungalows.

PRINCE NASTAVIA
You get a higher rent for a bungalow.

PRINCE NICEAVIA
The cottages were much nicer to look at.

PRINCE NASTAVIA
You can't stop the march of time.

PRINCE NICEAVIA
I'm sure you can if you want to.

We see an aerial view of the village. With the demolition of the cottages and the building of the bungalows, Wiffyville now shows a sad face.

PRINCE NASTAVIA
Have you got any money on you?

PRINCE NICEAVIA
That's typical. The one who has the most money never spends it.

PRINCE NASTAVIA
I'll pay you back.

PRINCE NICEAVIA
Famous last words. What do you want money for anyway?

PRINCE NASTAVIA
The telescope only works if you put a coin in the slot.

PRINCE NICEAVIA
How much do you need?

PRINCE NASTAVIA

A Wiffyville cent gives you five minutes.

PRINCE NICEAVIA rummages in his pockets and finds some coins. One of the coins is a shiny new one.

PRINCE NICEAVIA

Oh, look! It's one of the new cent coins with Lord Dippy Hughes on it.

PRINCE NASTAVIA grabs the coin.

PRINCE NASTAVIA

Just give it here.

PRINCE NASTAVIA pushes the coin into the slot beside the telescope and adjusts the focus.

With the aid of the telescope, PRINCE NASTAVIA sees GEOFFREY the giraffe's head sticking out from the top of the castle's tower. GEOFFREY the giraffe is staring back at him through his binoculars.

PRINCE NASTAVIA moves the telescope until he sees PRINCESS PUMPALOT in the distance through a castle window.

PRINCE NICEAVIA

Can you see anything?

PRINCE NASTAVIA

No . . . nothing much.

CUT TO:

INT. KING'S CHAMBERS - DAY

The KING, QUEEN and PRINCESS PUMPALOT are now sitting around a large wooden table.

                    KING
        On the occasion of your 13th birthday, I
        present you with the key to the cabinet.

                PRINCESS PUMPALOT
        The what?

                    KING
        The key to the cabinet.

The KING places a large key, attached to a piece of string, on the table.

                PRINCESS PUMPALOT
        I don't understand.

                    QUEEN
        Just listen to your father.

                PRINCESS PUMPALOT
        I am listening.

                    KING
        It is a tradition in our Royal Family to present
        any first child, whose 13th birthday lands on a
        Tuesday, the key to the cabinet.

21

PRINCESS PUMPALOT

And what is in this cabinet?

KING

The cabinet contains magic beans.

PRINCESS PUMPALOT

Magic beans? This gets weirder by the minute.

KING

The magic beans will provide you with powers
to help protect the castle from invasion.

PRINCESS PUMPALOT

Are you kidding? How does that work? Do I
plant them in the garden and wait for a beanstalk
to grow? Then we can all escape up it!

QUEEN

Sarcasm is the lowest form of wit, young lady.

PRINCESS PUMPALOT

At least I've got some.

There is an awkward silence.

KING

Look, you both need to show some humility
towards each other. This is an historic moment.
This is the first time for 400 years a first child's
13th birthday has fallen on a Tuesday.

The KING takes a map out of his waistcoat pocket and places it on the table.

                    KING (CONT'D)
      This map will show you the way to the cabinet.

                 PRINCESS PUMPALOT
      This doesn't make any sense.

                      QUEEN
      It makes perfect sense.

                 PRINCESS PUMPALOT
      What are these magic beans for?

The KING pauses for a moment.

                       KING
      The magic beans will make you fart.

                 PRINCESS PUMPALOT
      What?

                       KING
      They will make you fart.

                 PRINCESS PUMPALOT
      Are you serious?

                       KING
      Very serious.

                 PRINCESS PUMPALOT
      Why would I want to fart?

QUEEN

It's a tradition.

PRINCESS PUMPALOT
(sarcastically)
It's not very ladylike.

The KING is now angry.

KING

Look, this is serious. It's about the protection
of the castle from invasion. It should be an
honour to serve. Take the map.

PRINCESS PUMPALOT takes the map from the KING.

PRINCESS PUMPALOT

This is bonkers!

CUT TO:

INT. LORD DIPPY HUGHES'S LIBRARY - DAY

LORD DIPPY HUGHES is standing beside a bookshelf.
He is reading from a book. We see the title of the book,
'SCREENWRITING FOR BEGINNERS'.

LORD DIPPY HUGHES

It seems that when you're writing a screenplay,
you're only meant to use character names in
capital letters when they appear in the story for
the first time.

LORD DIPPY HUGHES coughs.

                    LORD DIPPY HUGHES (CONT'D)
          Oh, it doesn't matter. What's wrong with a little
          rule-breaking? I think it makes it easier to read.

LORD DIPPY HUGHES places the book down on the table
in front of him.

                                                    CUT TO:

INT. PRINCESS PUMPALOT'S BED CHAMBER - DAY

PRINCESS PUMPALOT has washed and changed her
clothes. She is now wearing a clean dress.

Her servant, GUFFY (13 years old), has the map in his hand.

PRINCESS PUMPALOT has the large key to the cabinet on a
piece of string around her neck.

                    PRINCESS PUMPALOT
          Guffy, I just don't see why I have to follow tradition.

                    GUFFY
          Some traditions are good to follow.

                    PRINCESS PUMPALOT
          Like what?

                    GUFFY
          Birthdays. Anniversaries. Weddings.

PRINCESS PUMPALOT

Yes, but not magic beans that make you fart.

GUFFY

There might be more to it than that.

PRINCESS PUMPALOT

I can't imagine what.

GUFFY

Look, let's just find this cabinet and take it from there.

CUT TO:

INT. CASTLE DUNGEONS - DAY

Holding a bright lantern, PRINCESS PUMPALOT ventures down into the dark dungeon with GUFFY, who is carrying the map.

PRINCESS PUMPALOT

Are you sure we're in the right section of the dungeon?

GUFFY

Yes, I think so.

GUFFY runs his finger over the map.

GUFFY (CONT'D)

Fourth on the right past the tunnel to Wiffyville. Third on the left after the cave symbols. And straight on for 89 yards past the purple wheelbarrow.

They hear a dripping sound.

                    PRINCESS PUMPALOT
          Quiet! I hear something.

                         GUFFY
          It's the drip.

                    PRINCESS PUMPALOT
          The drip?

                         GUFFY
          It says on the map that the drip will show us
          the way.

They follow the dripping sound until they reach a section of
the dungeon where water is dripping into a wooden barrel.

The dripping water creates an arrow shape in the barrel of
water.

                    GUFFY (CONT'D)
          Look, it's pointing us in the right direction.

                    PRINCESS PUMPALOT
          What if it's pointing us in the wrong direction?

                         GUFFY
          It's not what the map says. Come on.

They venture down another dark passage until they see light at
the end of the tunnel.

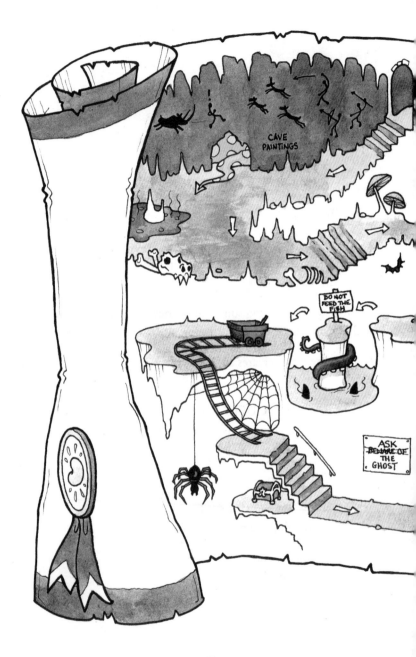

CAVE PAINTINGS

DO NOT FEED THE FISH

ASK BEWARE OF THE GHOST

DUNGEONS

TUNNEL TO WIFFYVILLE

ENTER FROM CASTLE

CERTAIN DEATH!

THE DRIP WILL SHOW YOU THE WAY

PURPLE WHEEL BARROW

N

W

S

FIRE EXIT

X MARKS THE SPOT!

GUFFY (CONT'D)
There's light at the end of the tunnel.

PRINCESS PUMPALOT
State the obvious.

GUFFY
The light is getting bigger.

PRINCESS PUMPALOT
Probably because we're walking towards it.

PRINCESS PUMPALOT and GUFFY reach the end of the tunnel and walk out into the village of Wiffyville.

CUT TO:

EXT. WIFFYVILLE VILLAGE - DAY

PRINCESS PUMPALOT stops.

PRINCESS PUMPALOT
I knew we were going the wrong way.

GUFFY
But the map says . . .

PRINCESS PUMPALOT grabs the map out of GUFFY'S hand.

PRINCESS PUMPALOT
Let me see it.
(reading)
The drip will show us the way P.T.O.

GUFFY

P.T.O?

PRINCESS PUMPALOT

P.T.O. It means, please turn over.

GUFFY turns his back and looks away from PRINCESS
PUMPALOT.

PRINCESS PUMPALOT (CONT'D)

Not you! The map.

PRINCESS PUMPALOT turns over the map to reveal the
continuation of the instructions.

PRINCESS PUMPALOT (CONT'D)

Guffy!
(reading)
The drip will show us the way . . .

PRINCESS PUMPALOT turns the page.

PRINCESS PUMPALOT (CONT'D)

. . . To Wiffyville.
(repeating)
The drip will show us the way to Wiffyville.

PRINCESS PUMPALOT shakes her head. GUFFY looks
sheepish.

GUFFY

Sorry.

PRINCESS PUMPALOT

For goodness sake. What a waste of time.

GUFFY

I'm really sorry.

PRINCESS PUMPALOT and GUFFY turn. As they do, they are met by a two-headed guard called LOOTS. He's carrying a tennis racket.

BOTH LOOTS'S heads speak at the same time. Unfortunately his right head speaks slower than his left head creating a strange echo.

LOOTS

Who goes there?

PRINCESS PUMPALOT

Oh hello, Loots.

LOOTS

Your Royal Highness.

LOOTS bows.

PRINCESS PUMPALOT

Have you been playing tennis?

LOOTS

Oh no. The King doesn't trust me to guard the tunnel with a spear, so he gave me a tennis racket instead. Let me show you my backhand.

33

LOOTS waves the tennis racket in a backhand motion. As he does, the tennis racket flies out of his hand and lands on the guardhouse roof.

LOOTS (CONT'D)
Oops. I'll get that down later.

GUFFY turns to PRINCESS PUMPALOT.

GUFFY
(whispering)
I can see why Sidney was promoted ahead of Loots.

LOOTS bends down and takes another tennis racket out of an old suitcase at his feet.

LOOTS
I've a few spares.

PRINCESS PUMPALOT smiles.

LOOTS (CONT'D)
So, what brings you to Wiffyville?

PRINCESS PUMPALOT
Guffy.

LOOTS turns to GUFFY.

LOOTS
What brings you to Wiffyville?

PRINCESS PUMPALOT
No, Loots! Guffy brought us to Wiffyville!

GUFFY shrugs his shoulders.

GUFFY
A wrong turning.

LOOTS
It happens.

PRINCESS PUMPALOT
Loots, we need to go back into the tunnel.

LOOTS moves forward brandishing his tennis racket.

LOOTS
(loudly)
What is your business in the castle?

PRINCESS PUMPALOT puts her arm around Loots's shoulder.

PRINCESS PUMPALOT
(quietly)
Loots. You know who we are. You only need to ask this question to strangers. You don't need to ask us.

LOOTS nods his head.

LOOTS
Oh yes. So I do. Sorry. On you go, Your Royal Highness.

35

PRINCESS PUMPALOT and GUFFY walk back into the tunnel.

CUT TO:

INT. CASTLE DUNGEONS - MOMENTS LATER

PRINCESS PUMPALOT and GUFFY walk further into the tunnel until they come to a dead end. It's a brick wall.

PRINCESS PUMPALOT
Not again!

GUFFY
I was sure we were going in the right direction.

GUFFY sighs and leans against the brick wall.

GUFFY (CONT'D)
I give up. I knew I should have used the Sat Nav on my phone.

Suddenly a ghostly head floating in mid-air appears from nowhere. It's a ghost called F.A.Q.

PRINCESS PUMPALOT and GUFFY are both startled.

PRINCESS PUMPALOT
What the . . .?

GUFFY
For goodness sake!

PRINCESS PUMPALOT and GUFFY slowly step back. F.A.Q moves towards them.

F.A.Q speaks with a low, booming voice.

F.A.Q

Don't be afraid.

PRINCESS PUMPALOT
You startled us.

F.A.Q
My apologies. It wasn't my intention.

PRINCESS PUMPALOT
Who are you?

F.A.Q

I am Fak.

PRINCESS PUMPALOT
Fak?

F.A.Q
My full name is Frequently Asked Questions
but my nickname is Fak.

PRINCESS PUMPALOT
Okay.

F.A.Q
I am the protector of the cabinet. Before
allowing you access to it, I must be sure that
you are furnished with all the necessary facts
pertaining to the magic beans.

GUFFY

Right.

F.A.Q

You must ask at least five of the top ten
frequently asked questions before venturing
further.

PRINCESS PUMPALOT

Like a quiz?

F.A.Q

Something like that. Although it's the questions
you need to get right, not the answers.

PRINCESS PUMPALOT

I see.

F.A.Q

I'm the all-seeing, all-hearing, legless ghoul.

GUFFY

I was wondering about that.
Where is the rest of your body?

PRINCESS PUMPALOT grabs GUFFY'S arm.

PRINCESS PUMPALOT

Guffy, I'm not sure you can ask a question
like that.

F.A.Q

I don't mind.

                    GUFFY
He doesn't mind.

                    F.A.Q
I had always wanted to be a headless horseman
but jobs like that are rare. So I became the
body-less, pony-less man.

                    GUFFY
        (slowly repeating)
The body-less, pony-less man.
And where do they dish out jobs like that?

                    F.A.Q
Wiffyville's Ghostly College of Spookery.

                    GUFFY
You learn something new every day.

                    F.A.Q
It's not all bad, though. I was lucky to get this
job 400 years ago.

              PRINCESS PUMPALOT
Have there been many intruders in that time?

                    F.A.Q
No. It's been fairly quiet, to be fair, until now
that is.

F.A.Q spins his head.

                    F.A.Q (CONT'D)
I'm rather excited. It's been a long wait. You
are the first people I have spoken to in four
centuries, so please, fire away.

                         GUFFY
Fire away? What do you mean?

                         F.A.Q
Ask some questions. That's what I'm here for.

               PRINCESS PUMPALOT
I thought that's what we were doing?

                         F.A.Q
Yes, but you've not asked any of the frequently
asked questions.

               PRINCESS PUMPALOT
Right.

PRINCESS PUMPALOT turns to GUFFY.

          PRINCESS PUMPALOT (CONT'D)
You go first.

                         GUFFY
No, you go first.

Both PRINCESS PUMPALOT and GUFFY fall silent. They
are not sure what to ask.

                          40

CUT TO:

INT. KING'S CHAMBERS - DAY

The QUEEN is reading from a book. We see the author's name, LORD DIPPY HUGHES.

                    QUEEN
          It's a double-edged sword.

                    KING
          What is?

                    QUEEN
          The magic beans.

                    KING
          Why?

                    QUEEN
          Although they will provide greater security for
          the castle and Wiffyville, they will also attract
          unnecessary attention.

                    KING
          Let's just wait and see.

The QUEEN places the book on the table.

                    QUEEN
          You're right. I'm not going to read any more
          of this book. It will just make me worry.

CUT TO:

INT. CASTLE DUNGEONS - DAY

PRINCESS PUMPALOT and GUFFY are standing in front of F.A.Q.

GUFFY has decided to ask the first question. He smiles and turns to F.A.Q.

GUFFY
How many tins of magic beans are there?

There is a bell sound and the number 1 appears floating in mid-air beside F.A.Q. PRINCESS PUMPALOT and GUFFY are startled.

F.A.Q
You're up and running. One out of five!

PRINCESS PUMPALOT
Good question, Guffy.

F.A.Q
There are 32,141 tins of magic beans. This represents a tin for every day until the Princess reaches 101 years of age.

GUFFY takes out his mobile phone from his pocket and switches on the calculator. He starts tapping away on the keypad.

42

                    PRINCESS PUMPALOT
What are you doing?

                         GUFFY
I'm going to work it out.

                    PRINCESS PUMPALOT
Work what out?

                         GUFFY
How many tins of magic beans there should be.

                    PRINCESS PUMPALOT
Fak just told us!

                         GUFFY
I want to work it out for myself.

PRINCESS PUMPALOT looks at F.A.Q and shrugs her
shoulders.

                    GUFFY (CONT'D)
        101 years minus 13 years equals 88 years.
        Multiply 88 years by 365 days in the year and
        that equals 32,120 tins of magic beans.

GUFFY turns to F.A.Q.

                    GUFFY (CONT'D)
        Fak, I think you've got the figure wrong. It
        should be 32,120 tins of magic beans.

F.A.Q

My dear Guffy. You have missed out leap years in your calculations.

GUFFY looks deflated.

GUFFY

I didn't think of that.

F.A.Q

Every four years we have an extra day in the year, 366 days instead of 365. The extra day is on the 29th February. From now until the Princess reaches 101 years of age, there will be 21 leap years. So, the total is 32,141 tins of magic beans.

GUFFY looks confused.

GUFFY

Wait a minute. Surely it's 22 leap years from now until the Princess reaches 101? 13 years plus 88 years is 101 years.

F.A.Q

That is correct.

GUFFY

Therefore 88 divided by four is 22.

F.A.Q

That is also correct.

                                GUFFY
             So, it's 22 leap years. Not 21. Making it a
             grand total of 32,142 tins of magic beans.

GUFFY looks pleased with himself. PRINCESS PUMPALOT
is getting bored.

                                F.A.Q
             Not quite, Guffy. Leap years are indeed every
             four years, such as 2016 and 2020. However,
             leap years do not occur in years that are evenly
             divisible by 100, with the exception of those
             that are divisible by 400. This means that the
             year 2000 was a leap year but the year 2100
             will not be a leap year.

Suddenly F.A.Q, PRINCESS PUMPALOT and GUFFY
freeze as if someone has pressed the pause button on a remote
control.

                                                    CUT TO:

INT. LORD DIPPY HUGHES'S LIBRARY - DAY

LORD DIPPY HUGHES is standing beside a bookshelf. He
is reading from a book. We see the title of the book, 'LEAP
YEARS FOR PEOPLE INTERESTED IN LEAP YEARS'.

                        LORD DIPPY HUGHES
             Let me just interject here. A leap year is
             necessary to keep the calendar year in sync with
             the seasons. While the calendar assumes the

                                  45

LORD DIPPY HUGHES (CONT'D)
earth revolves around the sun every 365 days, it
actually takes longer; something like 365 days,
5 hours, 48 minutes and 46 seconds. If we
didn't have leap years, the calendar would be
off by approximately 24 days every 100 years
and our seasons would be all over the place.

LORD DIPPY HUGHES looks up.

LORD DIPPY HUGHES (CONT'D)
You got it?

LORD DIPPY HUGHES places the book down on the table
in front of him.

CUT TO:

INT. CASTLE DUNGEONS - DAY

GUFFY has his hands in his pockets.

F.A.Q
So it's 32,141 tins of magic beans. Happy now,
Guffy?

GUFFY

Suppose.

PRINCESS PUMPALOT stares at F.A.Q.

PRINCESS PUMPALOT
Surely I don't have to eat magic beans every day?

F.A.Q

Oh no. Definitely not. That would be dangerous. You only need to eat them when there's an invasion.

PRINCESS PUMPALOT

And when will that happen?

F.A.Q

Invaders don't tend to tell you when they're going to invade.

GUFFY

Makes sense.

PRINCESS PUMPALOT

What actually happens when I eat the magic beans?

There is a bell sound and the number 2 appears floating in mid-air beside F.A.Q.

F.A.Q

You'll have to wait and see.

PRINCESS PUMPALOT

Wait and see. That's not a clear answer.

F.A.Q

It's an answer.

GUFFY

He has a point. It is an answer.

47

PRINCESS PUMPALOT turns to GUFFY.

PRINCESS PUMPALOT
But he didn't answer the question.

GUFFY
Yes, he did.

PRINCESS PUMPALOT turns to F.A.Q.

PRINCESS PUMPALOT
I thought you were here to help?

F.A.Q
I am. It's just there are certain things I can't say.
It's tradition.

PRINCESS PUMPALOT sighs.

PRINCESS PUMPALOT
Tradition! Tradition! Tradition! I'm fed up
hearing that word.

GUFFY
You shouldn't say it three times, then!

PRINCESS PUMPALOT makes a funny face at GUFFY.

PRINCESS PUMPALOT
Funny.

F.A.Q
Look, can we get back on to the questions, please?

PRINCESS PUMPALOT folds her arms.

PRINCESS PUMPALOT
Why have I never heard about the magic beans
and why did my family keep this a secret from
me for 13 years?

There is a bell sound and the numbers 3 and 4 appear floating
in mid-air on either side of F.A.Q.

GUFFY
Wow! Two questions in one. Very impressive.

F.A.Q
The King and Queen were sworn to secrecy
when they realised the significance of their first
child reaching 13 years of age on a Tuesday.
A book written by Lord Dippy Hughes,
discovered in the Royal Archives, reveals that
the village of Wiffyville was cursed by a bearded
witch and would disappear without trace if the
Princess was told about the magic beans before
her 13th birthday.

49

GUFFY

The village or the witch?

F.A.Q

The village or the witch, what?

GUFFY

What would disappear? The village or the witch?

F.A.Q

The village, of course! Why would a witch
make herself disappear?

GUFFY shrugs his shoulders.

GUFFY

But you said, 'Wiffyville was cursed by a
bearded witch and would disappear without
trace'. It's not clear if it's the village or the witch
that would disappear. It's a little ambiguous.

PRINCESS PUMPALOT
(jokingly)
Ooh! Ambiguous. Big word for Guffy.

GUFFY makes a face at PRINCESS PUMPALOT.

F.A.Q
Okay! Okay! For Guffy's benefit, let me add
some clarity to my statement.

F.A.Q clears his throat.

F.A.Q (CONT'D)
A book written by Lord Dippy Hughes,
discovered in the Royal Archives, reveals that
the village of Wiffyville was cursed by a
bearded witch and
    (pause)
the village would disappear without trace if the
Princess was told about the magic beans before
her 13th birthday. Is that better?

GUFFY
Much better.

F.A.Q shakes his head.

PRINCESS PUMPALOT
How was the witch planning to make the
village disappear?

F.A.Q
There would be 12 days and nights of rain.
The lake would overflow and the town of
Wiffyville would be washed away forever.
    (pause)
But thankfully that won't happen now as the
secret has been kept intact. Glory be!

F.A.Q in his excitement bounces his head on the ground like
a football.

F.A.Q (CONT'D)

Right, you only need to ask one more
frequently asked question and you'll get to see
inside the cabinet.

PRINCESS PUMPALOT

I don't see any cabinet.

F.A.Q

All will be revealed.

There is a short silence. PRINCESS PUMPALOT stares at
GUFFY. They are not sure what to ask.

F.A.Q (CONT'D)

Do you want a clue?

PRINCESS PUMPALOT

That might help.

F.A.Q clears his throat.

F.A.Q

The clue is . . . a bobcat mice intention hot.

There is another short silence.

GUFFY

Sounds like a cryptic clue.

PRINCESS PUMPALOT

I'm hopeless with cryptic clues. I even have
difficulty with the easy crossword in the
Wiffyville Gazette.

GUFFY

I won the Gazette's crossword competition
two years ago. They sent me a book token.

PRINCESS PUMPALOT

You should be able to work this out then.

GUFFY

(slowly)
A bobcat mice intention hot.

GUFFY scratches his head.

GUFFY (CONT'D)

Em, a bobcat is probably a kind of cat and cats
chase mice or intend to chase mice.

PRINCESS PUMPALOT

There are mice in the castle.

GUFFY

I know, but where does the word hot fit in.

There is a long pause.

CUT TO:

INT. CASTLE DUNGEONS - 15 MINUTES LATER

PRINCESS PUMPALOT and GUFFY are still trying to work
out the answer to F.A.Q's clue.

PRINCESS PUMPALOT

Cat on a hot tin roof?

                    GUFFY
What does that mean?

                PRINCESS PUMPALOT
It's a book I've seen on a shelf in the castle library.

                    GUFFY
What's it about?

                PRINCESS PUMPALOT
I don't know. A cat, I suppose.

                                        CUT TO:

INT. CASTLE DUNGEONS - 20 MINUTES LATER

PRINCESS PUMPALOT and GUFFY are still trying to work
out the answer to F.A.Q's clue.

                PRINCESS PUMPALOT
        So if Bob in the village has a cat and the cat
        chases mice, Bob or the cat will be running a
        lot and will get really hot. It will be like a hot
        dog except it will be a hot cat.

F.A.Q is bemused by this explanation.

                    GUFFY
        But what about the word, intention? With these
        sorts of clues, you need to use all the words.

                PRINCESS PUMPALOT
        Maybe if we bring a cat down here it will lead
        us to the . . .

                        54

PRINCESS PUMPALOT isn't sure what to say next.

PRINCESS PUMPALOT (CONT'D)
It could be an anagram.

GUFFY looks at PRINCESS PUMPALOT and smiles.

GUFFY
I think you could be right! It's an anagram.

GUFFY takes out his mobile phone.

GUFFY (CONT'D)
I'll just check it on my anagram app.

GUFFY types A BOBCAT MICE INTENTION HOT on his phone's keypad. PRINCESS PUMPALOT and F.A.Q stare over his shoulder. GUFFY scrolls down the list of anagrams.

F.A.Q
That's a clever machine.

GUFFY
It's called a Smartphone.

F.A.Q
It must be very smart if it can mix words up to create new words.

PRINCESS PUMPALOT
It does a lot more than that, Fak.

GUFFY points at the screen.

55

                              GUFFY
        There it is.

                       PRINCESS PUMPALOT
                          (reading)
        A cabbie ethnic tomtit noon.

GUFFY points at the correct anagram.

                              GUFFY
        No, underneath that one!

                       PRINCESS PUMPALOT
                          (reading)
        Combination to the cabinet.

Several bells sound and the number 5 appears floating in
mid-air. Then the numbers 1, 2, 3 and 4 arrange themselves in
numerical order beside number 5.

                  PRINCESS PUMPALOT (CONT'D)
        Well done, Guffy!

                                56

F.A.Q

1, 2, 3, 4 and 5. The combination to the cabinet.

GUFFY

Brilliant! No-one would ever guess that
combination.

F.A.Q

Ah, you may mock me but the brilliance of
this combination is in its simplicity.

GUFFY is not convinced.

GUFFY

If you say so.

F.A.Q spins his head again.

The numbers 1, 2, 3, 4 and 5 are still floating in mid-air.

F.A.Q

Right, all you need to do now is punch the
numbers.

PRINCESS PUMPALOT

You mean punch in the numbers.

F.A.Q

No, I mean punch the numbers. Don't worry;
they don't feel anything.

With his mouth, F.A.Q picks up a pair of boxing gloves from
the ground and passes them to PRINCESS PUMPALOT.

57

PRINCESS PUMPALOT puts on the boxing gloves and punches the numbers 1, 2, 3, 4 and 5.

Each time a number is punched it disappears inside a crack in the wall. When the number 5 disappears, the bricks in the wall pop out, one by one.

PRINCESS PUMPALOT and GUFFY dive on the ground.

F.A.Q (CONT'D)
I forgot to say. Watch out for flying bricks!

PRINCESS PUMPALOT
This is information we could have done with earlier!

Once they feel it's safe, PRINCESS PUMPALOT and GUFFY look up and stare at a large wooden cabinet in front of a pile of bricks.

Magically, the cabinet doors swing open, revealing 32,141 tins of magic beans.

PRINCESS PUMPALOT (CONT'D)
How extraordinary!

GUFFY
For goodness sake.

58

PRINCESS PUMPALOT
They are so beautifully stacked.

F.A.Q
The tins are arranged in rows by BEST
BEFORE dates.

GUFFY

I suppose it's no good arranging the beans in alphabetical order.

F.A.Q

Guffy, you are a very silly boy.

PRINCESS PUMPALOT laughs.

PRINCESS PUMPALOT

That's quite funny.

F.A.Q picks out a tin of magic beans with his mouth and places it on the ground in front of PRINCESS PUMPALOT.

F.A.Q

You must now eat your first magic bean.

GUFFY

Probably tradition?

F.A.Q

It is indeed.

There is a tin opener hanging on the inside of the cabinet door. F.A.Q passes the tin opener to GUFFY.

GUFFY

You want me to do the honours?

F.A.Q

I do.

GUFFY opens a tin of magic beans and hands the tin to PRINCESS PUMPALOT. Inside the tin, there are two compartments, one with green beans and the other with red beans.

PRINCESS PUMPALOT
They're different colours.

F.A.Q
Try the red one first. Remember to bend over.

PRINCESS PUMPALOT eats one of the red beans and bends over. There is a gurgling noise and Phhhhhhhart - the cabinet door is blown off its hinges by a gusty fart.

PRINCESS PUMPALOT
That is brilliant!

GUFFY

Wow! All right!

PRINCESS PUMPALOT

Quite extraordinary. I never knew farting
could be such fun.

F.A.Q stares at the cabinet door lying on the ground.

GUFFY

Here's a good question. Can anyone apart
from the Princess gain powers from eating the
magic beans?

F.A.Q

The magic beans can be eaten by someone else,
but that someone else will only gain extra
powers if they also hold the key to the cabinet.
So the key is the key.

PRINCESS PUMPALOT

No pun intended.

F.A.Q smiles.

GUFFY

But surely if someone has the key to the cabinet
all they have to do is open the cabinet . . .
with the key.

F.A.Q

Oh no! You should never use the key to open
the cabinet. Never! The only person who can

F.A.Q (CONT'D)

use the key to open the cabinet is the Princess.
If anyone else opens the cabinet with the key,
they will turn into a mouse.

GUFFY

A mouse?

F.A.Q

The magic beans therefore need to
stay in the cabinet until they are
required and the cabinet needs to
remain locked. Once I fix the
cabinet door, that is.

GUFFY

What about the bricks?

F.A.Q

The cabinet will no longer be hidden by bricks.

PRINCESS PUMPALOT waves the key to the cabinet in
front of GUFFY.

GUFFY

Keep that key away from me. I like mice but I
wouldn't want to be one.

Suddenly F.A.Q, PRINCESS PUMPALOT and GUFFY
freeze as if someone has pressed the pause button on a remote
control.

CUT TO:

INT. LORD DIPPY HUGHES'S LIBRARY - DAY

LORD DIPPY HUGHES is sitting in a comfy armchair, with a large dusty book open in front of him. He is dressed as a clown.

> LORD DIPPY HUGHES
> Sorry to interrupt the story again but I feel it's important to clarify the rules relating to the key to the cabinet. If I leave Fak to explain everything, I fear that we'll be here all night.

LORD DIPPY HUGHES turns a page in his book.

> LORD DIPPY HUGHES (CONT'D)
> The Princess can use the key to open the cabinet but no-one else can, unless they want to be turned into a mouse. However, anyone can lock the cabinet.

LORD DIPPY HUGHES scratches his nose.

> LORD DIPPY HUGHES (CONT'D)
> Someone other than the Princess can only gain the powers if they hold the key to the cabinet and a tin of magic beans at the same time. The Princess, however, does not have to be holding the key to the cabinet for the magic beans to work for her. Is that clear?

LORD DIPPY HUGHES stares ahead.

                    LORD DIPPY HUGHES (CONT'D)
          Right, let's get back to the story.

                                        CUT TO:

EXT. CASTLE GROUNDS - LATER

PRINCESS PUMPALOT has a tin of magic beans in her left
hand. GUFFY is a metre away from her. There is a safety net
perched up against the castle wall.

                    PRINCESS PUMPALOT
          Right, stand there. Don't move.

                    GUFFY
          Remember it's the red bean not the green one.

                    PRINCESS PUMPALOT
          I know what I'm doing.

PRINCESS PUMPALOT eats one of the red beans and bends
over. There is a gurgling noise and Phhhhhhart - GUFFY is
blown past the safety net and over the castle ramparts.

PRINCESS PUMPALOT looks around.

                    PRINCESS PUMPALOT (CONT'D)
          Oh no! What have I done?

GUFFY is nowhere to be seen.

                    PRINCESS PUMPALOT (CONT'D)
                 Guffy?

There is no reply.

                    PRINCESS PUMPALOT (CONT'D)
                    (shouting)
                 Guffy!

                              GUFFY

            Help!

PRINCESS PUMPALOT runs to the castle ramparts, looks
over and sees GUFFY hanging on a jagged rock.

                         GUFFY (CONT'D)
                 Help! Help me!

PRINCESS PUMPALOT reaches over the castle ramparts and
pushes her hand forward.

                       PRINCESS PUMPALOT
                 Take my hand.

GUFFY manages to grab hold of PRINCESS PUMPALOT'S
hand and he is pulled back over the ramparts to safety.

                    PRINCESS PUMPALOT (CONT'D)
                 Wow! I think we need to take care with these
                 magic beans.

                              GUFFY
            You saved my life!

                               66

CUT TO:

EXT. TOP OF GOTHIC TOWER, WIFFYVILLE - DAY

Twin brothers PRINCE NASTAVIA and PRINCE
NICEAVIA are still on their roof garden.

PRINCE NICEAVIA sits at a table with a pencil in his hand.
He is drawing a sketch of PRINCESS PUMPALOT.

PRINCE NASTAVIA is looking through the telescope. He is
watching PRINCESS PUMPALOT and GUFFY.

> PRINCE NASTAVIA
> My goodness, that is a powerful weapon.

> PRINCE NICEAVIA
> What is?

> PRINCE NASTAVIA
> The em . . .

PRINCE NASTAVIA moves away from the telescope and tries
to think of something to say.

> PRINCE NASTAVIA (CONT'D)
> . . . the big cannon.

> PRINCE NICEAVIA
> Oh yes, the big cannon can fire a cannonball
> four miles.

PRINCE NASTAVIA tries to sound interested.

67

PRINCE NASTAVIA
Really? Four miles? That is a long way.

PRINCE NASTAVIA sits down at the table and sends a text from his mobile phone.

PRINCE NICEAVIA
I'm thinking about doing a painting for the Princess's birthday. The trouble is, there are so many portraits hanging in the castle, they might not have room for another one. What do you think?

PRINCE NASTAVIA
I could ask the King when I see him this afternoon.

PRINCE NICEAVIA
You're seeing the King this afternoon?

PRINCE NASTAVIA
I am. And the Queen.

PRINCE NICEAVIA
Why?

PRINCE NASTAVIA
To ask if I can take Princess Pumpalot to the Royal Birthday Ball.

PRINCE NICEAVIA is shocked. He stands up.

PRINCE NICEAVIA
What? You can't do that!

PRINCE NASTAVIA
Why not?

PRINCE NICEAVIA
Because I want to take the Princess to the
Royal Birthday Ball.

PRINCE NASTAVIA
Have you asked her?

PRINCE NICEAVIA
No.

PRINCE NASTAVIA
Then I'm going to ask her.

PRINCE NICEAVIA
I want to ask her.

PRINCE NASTAVIA
Wanting and doing are two very different
things.

PRINCE NICEAVIA
But you know how much I like her.

PRINCE NASTAVIA
So what.

PRINCE NICEAVIA
You've never shown a blind bit of interest in
her until now.

PRINCE NASTAVIA
And your point is?

PRINCE NICEAVIA
Why now?

PRINCE NASTAVIA pictures in his head PRINCESS
PUMPALOT farting and blowing GUFFY over the castle
ramparts.

PRINCE NASTAVIA
There's something I see in her that's very
attractive.

PRINCE NICEAVIA
Well, if you're going to see the King and
Queen, so am I.

CUT TO:

INT. PRINCESS PUMPALOT'S BED CHAMBER - DAY

PRINCESS PUMPALOT and GUFFY are staring into an
open tin of magic beans.

PRINCESS PUMPALOT
Fak didn't say anything about the green beans.
I suppose there's only one way to find out.

GUFFY

I think I'll stay well clear this time, if you don't
mind.

GUFFY moves to the other side of the room and pushes his
back against the wall.

PRINCESS PUMPALOT picks out a green bean from the tin
with her hand. The bean has a green wrapper around it.

PRINCESS PUMPALOT

It has a wrapper on it. It's like a sweetie wrapper.

GUFFY

I didn't notice that.

PRINCESS PUMPALOT unwraps the green bean. There are
words written on the back of the wrapper.

PRINCESS PUMPALOT

It says . . .
        (reading)
no need to bend down.

GUFFY

Is that all it says?

PRINCESS PUMPALOT

Yes.

GUFFY

Well, no need to bend down, then.

PRINCESS PUMPALOT eats the green bean. There is no noise. It's a silent fart. There is a smell. A strong smell. The smell is so strong, GUFFY faints and lands face down on the floor.

PRINCESS PUMPALOT
Oh, Guffy! What have I done?

PRINCESS PUMPALOT picks up a glass of water from the bedside table and throws it over GUFFY'S face.

PRINCESS PUMPALOT (CONT'D)
Are you okay?

GUFFY opens his eyes.

GUFFY
Yes, I'm fine, if a little wet.

PRINCESS PUMPALOT
Thank goodness.

GUFFY screws up his face.

GUFFY
That fart stinks!

CUT TO:

EXT. WIFFYVILLE VILLAGE - DAY

PRINCE NASTAVIA and PRINCE NICEAVIA walk briskly through the village.

They pass a STREET VENDOR selling newspapers. They don't notice the headline on his news board: 'TELESCOPE STOLEN FROM VILLAGE OBSERVATORY'.

They reach the entrance to the castle tunnel. LOOTS, the two-headed guard, steps forward, brandishing his tennis racket.

> LOOTS
> Who goes there?

> PRINCE NASTAVIA
> Prince Nastavia.

> LOOTS
> What is your business in the castle?

> PRINCE NASTAVIA
> I have an appointment with the King.

> LOOTS
> And what is the password?

> PRINCE NASTAVIA
> I don't know. I wasn't given one.

> LOOTS
> Actually, I don't know it either. On you go.

LOOTS waves him through. PRINCE NASTAVIA enters the tunnel. PRINCE NICEAVIA attempts to follow him but LOOTS stops him with his tennis racket.

> LOOTS (CONT'D)
> What is your business in the castle?

PRINCE NICEAVIA points at PRINCE NASTAVIA.

                    PRINCE NICEAVIA
    I'm with him.

LOOTS pauses for a second.

                         LOOTS
    On you go, then.

PRINCE NICEAVIA follows his brother into the tunnel.

                    PRINCE NICEAVIA
    Great security!

                                        CUT TO:

EXT. CASTLE GATE - DAY

PRINCE NASTAVIA and PRINCE NICEAVIA march out
of the tunnel and through the castle gates. They briskly walk
towards the King's Chambers.

They walk past PRINCESS PUMPALOT and GUFFY.

PRINCE NASTAVIA is looking straight ahead. PRINCE
NICEAVIA looks over to PRINCESS PUMPALOT and
smiles.

                   PRINCESS PUMPALOT
    Where are you going?

                    PRINCE NICEAVIA
    To see the King.

                    PRINCESS PUMPALOT
    Why?

PRINCESS PUMPALOT follows them.

                    PRINCE NICEAVIA
    Let's just say, I'm here for you.

PRINCE NASTAVIA turns his head towards PRINCESS
PUMPALOT.

                    PRINCE NASTAVIA
    He means I'm here for you.

PRINCESS PUMPALOT stops in her tracks.

PRINCE NASTAVIA and PRINCE NICEAVIA enter the
King's Chambers.

PRINCESS PUMPALOT enters the bed chamber adjoining
the King's Chambers.

                                            CUT TO:

INT. BED CHAMBER - DAY

PRINCESS PUMPALOT stands on a four-poster bed and
moves a painting from the wall.

There are two holes in the wall. These holes are eyeholes which
match up with a painting on the adjoining wall in the King's
Chambers. The painting is of the Queen's mother holding a
cat on her knee. The eyeholes match up with the cat's eyes.

From the eyeholes, PRINCESS PUMPALOT can see and hear everything the KING and QUEEN are saying.

KING

This is very short notice.

QUEEN

He made an appointment by text.

KING

Who did?

QUEEN

Prince Nastavia.

KING

And what about his brother?

QUEEN

He's turned up without an appointment, which frankly is just plain rude. What is the world coming to when people blatantly disregard royal protocol?

KING

I presume we should still see him, though?

QUEEN

I suppose so, but he'll have to do a lot to impress me.

INT. WAITING AREA - DAY

PRINCE NASTAVIA and PRINCE NICEAVIA sit beside each other in silence.

CUT TO:

INT. KING'S CHAMBERS - DAY

The cat's eyes are moving in the painting on the wall.

There is a knock on the door.

SIDNEY the servant approaches the door. As he attempts to open the door, he drops his keys on the floor. The QUEEN shakes her head.

SIDNEY the servant opens the door to reveal a pair of giraffe legs on the other side of the door.

A small hatch in the ceiling opens. GEOFFREY the giraffe sticks his head through the hatch. He bows his head towards the KING and the QUEEN.

                    GEOFFREY
    Your Majesties, may I present Prince Nastavia?

PRINCE NASTAVIA marches into the room and bows.

                 PRINCE NASTAVIA
    Your Majesties.

                      KING
    Prince Nastavia. How can we help you this
    fine day?

PRINCE NASTAVIA
(confidently)
I would like your permission to escort the
Princess to the Royal Birthday Ball.

There is a gasp from behind the painting.

The KING and QUEEN look at each other.

KING
We have mice.

QUEEN
I am sorry.

KING
Do continue.

PRINCE NASTAVIA
Your Majesties. If you allow me to escort
Princess Pumpalot to the Ball, as a gesture of
goodwill I can offer you 24 cows, 18 tubs of
ice-cream and a guinea pig.

The QUEEN looks impressed.

QUEEN
May I ask the make of ice-cream?

PRINCE NASTAVIA smiles.

PRINCE NASTAVIA
Yes, Your Majesty. The ice-cream is homemade
by the famous Antonio triplets of Wiffyville.

80

PRINCE NASTAVIA (CONT'D)
I can arrange for a mix of flavours to be
especially created for your pleasure.

The QUEEN smiles.

QUEEN
Chocolate sorbet?

PRINCE NASTAVIA
Any flavour you'd like, Your Majesty.

KING
Well, thank you, Prince Nastavia. That is a
generous offer. We shall let you know our
answer in due course. Send your brother in on
the way out.

PRINCE NASTAVIA exits. PRINCE NICEAVIA enters the
King's Chambers and bows.

PRINCE NICEAVIA
Your Majesties.

KING
And what can we do for you, Prince Niceavia?

PRINCE NICEAVIA
I'm not sure how to say this.

KING
Take your time.

PRINCE NICEAVIA is very nervous. He takes a deep breath.

PRINCE NICEAVIA
I would like to ask your permission to escort
Princess Pumpalot to the Royal Birthday Ball.
I have for many months admired the Princess
from afar.

There is a cough from behind the painting.

QUEEN
We have mice.

KING
I do apologise.

QUEEN
Your brother seems to be doing well. Are you
involved in similar ventures?

PRINCE NICEAVIA
No, Your Majesty.

QUEEN
Oh. That is disappointing.

PRINCE NICEAVIA doesn't know what to say next. The
KING steps forward.

KING
What do you do in your spare time?

PRINCE NICEAVIA
Em, sketching and painting. I've held an exhibition of my work in Wiffyville's Town Hall. I sell the occasional portrait but they don't make me much money.

KING
How interesting.

QUEEN
Do you have anything to offer?

PRINCE NICEAVIA
I've been working on a portrait of the Princess.

QUEEN
Is that all! The castle doesn't need . . .

The KING interrupts.

KING
It's a nice thought, Prince Niceavia.

QUEEN
So, no ice-cream?

PRINCE NICEAVIA
I'm afraid not.

QUEEN
Cows? Guinea pigs?

PRINCE NICEAVIA
Neither.

The QUEEN is not impressed.

                    KING
          Thank you, Prince Niceavia. Please wait in the
          other room and we will inform you of our
          decision in due course.

PRINCE NICEAVIA bows and leaves the room. The KING
turns to the QUEEN.

                 KING (CONT'D)
          What do you think?

                   QUEEN
          There's no contest. Obviously Prince Nastavia
          is the better candidate.

                    KING
          But Prince Niceavia seems a genuine soul. I
          like his artistic side, and the portrait is a kind
          thing to offer.

                   QUEEN
          This castle doesn't need any more portraits.

The KING sighs and folds his arms.

                    KING
          I must say, I do like the sound of 24 new cows.

The KING pauses to think for a moment.

                    KING (CONT'D)
          You're right, my dear. We shall accept Prince
          Nastavia's offer.

There is a cry of 'NO' from behind the painting.

                    QUEEN
          You better phone the mouse catcher. That
          sounds like a big one.

                                              CUT TO:

EXT. CASTLE GROUNDS - MOMENTS LATER

PRINCESS PUMPALOT runs into the castle grounds. She
sees GUFFY in the distance.

               PRINCESS PUMPALOT
          Guffy! Guffy!

GUFFY turns and runs towards PRINCESS PUMPALOT.

                    GUFFY
          What's wrong?

               PRINCESS PUMPALOT
          It's the King and Queen.

                    GUFFY
          What's happened?

               PRINCESS PUMPALOT
          The Ball!

GUFFY

What about it?

PRINCESS PUMPALOT

They've arranged for me to go to the Royal
Birthday Ball with Prince Nastavia.

GUFFY

What?

PRINCESS PUMPALOT

How could they do such a thing?

Suddenly their conversation is interrupted by GEOFFREY the
giraffe. He is staring through his binoculars.

GEOFFREY

Warning! Warning! On the horizon I can see
low-flying gnomes. Take cover!

In the distance are 20 low-flying GNOMES. They're all
carrying bows and arrows.

GEOFFREY (CONT'D)

Gnomi che volano a bassa quota.

PRINCESS PUMPALOT

Eh? What did he say?

GUFFY

Sounds like Italian.

PRINCE NASTAVIA runs out into the courtyard. He sees the

low-flying GNOMES and hides behind a pillar.

PRINCE NICEAVIA rushes out into the courtyard.

> PRINCE NICEAVIA
> Can I help?

> GUFFY
> Yes. Fetch the Princess's magic beans.

> PRINCE NICEAVIA
> Magic beans?

> GUFFY
> Yes. There's a tin beside the battlements. And
> bring the tin opener.

PRINCE NICEAVIA collects the tin of magic beans and the tin opener. GUFFY opens the tin and turns to PRINCESS PUMPALOT.

> GUFFY (CONT'D)
> Get one of these down you.

The low-flying GNOMES are now hovering threateningly above the castle.

PRINCESS PUMPALOT eats one of the red beans and bends over. There is a gurgling noise and Phhhhhhhart - one of the GNOMES is blown out of the sky by a gusty fart.

> GUFFY (CONT'D)
> Good shot!

PRINCE NICEAVIA, watching this, is stunned.

                    PRINCE NICEAVIA
          Well, I never . . .

Before PRINCE NICEAVIA can finish his sentence, an arrow
lands only a few inches away from his right leg.

Annoyed by this, PRINCE NICEAVIA picks up the tin of
magic beans and throws it at one of the low-flying GNOMES.
He hits the low-flying GNOME right between the eyes.

Luckily the tin of magic beans drops to the ground and lands
upright beside PRINCESS PUMPALOT.

                    PRINCESS PUMPALOT
          Good shot . . . but they're for eating, not
          throwing.

PRINCESS PUMPALOT eats another one of the red beans
and bends over. There is a gurgling noise and Phhhhhhhart -
another low-flying GNOME is blown out of the sky.

The battle is in full flow.

GUFFY is kicking rugby balls at the low-flying GNOMES.

GEOFFREY the giraffe knocks out a low-flying GNOME
with his head.

The KING is on top of the tower with his catapult. He is
firing the QUEEN'S shoes at the low-flying GNOMES,
much to the QUEEN'S displeasure.

PRINCE NICEAVIA has found a fire hose. He is spraying the low-flying GNOMES with water.

SIDNEY the servant runs into the courtyard but falls over his shoe laces.

One of the low-flying GNOMES fires an arrow. It's heading towards PRINCESS PUMPALOT. GUFFY sees this and throws himself in front of PRINCESS PUMPALOT, saving her from injury. The arrow lands in GUFFY'S hair.

GUFFY stands up. He looks funny with an arrow through his hair.

PRINCESS PUMPALOT (CONT'D)
You saved my life!

PRINCESS PUMPALOT eats another red bean and bends over. There is a gurgling noise and Phhhhhhart - a low-flying GNOME is blown into two other low-flying GNOMES by another gusty fart. All three fall out of the sky.

The GNOMES retreat.

There is a loud cheer from the castle.

Everyone was so busy fighting, they didn't notice that PRINCE NASTAVIA was hiding.

PRINCE NASTAVIA ruffles his hair. He runs out from behind the pillar. He's pretending to have taken part in the battle.

PRINCE NASTAVIA
Oh, that was a close one. Well done, everyone.
I think I hit two or three low-flying gnomes.

GUFFY
I didn't see that.

PRINCE NASTAVIA
A couple of arrows nearly hit me too.

GUFFY
I didn't see that either.

PRINCE NASTAVIA approaches PRINCESS PUMPALOT.

PRINCE NASTAVIA
Is my Royal Birthday Ball partner okay?

PRINCESS PUMPALOT stares at him, doesn't say a word
and runs towards the dungeons. She is followed by GUFFY.

CUT TO:

INT. CASTLE DUNGEONS - LATER

PRINCESS PUMPALOT, holding a bright lantern, runs
down into the dark dungeon followed by GUFFY.

They chat while running.

PRINCESS PUMPALOT
Fak is bound to know what to do.

GUFFY
Not necessarily. He may not have any control
over whom you go to the Royal Birthday Ball
with.

PRINCESS PUMPALOT
Surely this can't be allowed to happen.

GUFFY
But if the King and Queen have made a
decision, you'll have to go along with it?

PRINCESS PUMPALOT
Not if I can help it.

GUFFY and PRINCESS PUMPALOT stop at a crossroads of tunnels, and then continue walking.

> GUFFY
> I'm sure the cabinet is this way.

> PRINCESS PUMPALOT
> I've heard you say this before. Where's the map?

> GUFFY
> One of the low-flying gnomes snatched it out
> of my pocket when we were fighting.

PRINCESS PUMPALOT stops in her tracks.

> PRINCESS PUMPALOT
> Oh no. That means the low-flying gnomes
> will know how to find the cabinet.

> GUFFY
> Yes, but remember, the magic beans are no
> good to them unless they also have the key to
> the cabinet.

PRINCESS PUMPALOT touches her neck to make sure the key to the cabinet is still there. It is.

> PRINCESS PUMPALOT
> I suppose.

GUFFY points.

GUFFY

There's the cabinet.

Suddenly F.A.Q appears floating in mid-air.

GUFFY (CONT'D)

And here's an old head on young . . . well, an old head.

PRINCESS PUMPALOT

Fak. Thank goodness. I need your help.

F.A.Q

Don't tell me. It's about Prince Nastavia.

PRINCESS PUMPALOT

How do you know that?

F.A.Q

I know everything. Well, I say I know everything. There are some modern inventions I'm not so familiar with. Apart from that, my general knowledge holds up well at the Ghouls Annual Debating Society Dinner Dance.

GUFFY

I suppose, when dancing, there's no chance of you stepping on someone's toes.

F.A.Q

I'll have you know I'm a great dancer, and don't worry, Princess Pumpalot, I can help you.

Magically, we hear music. It echoes through the dungeon. F.A.Q shows off his dance routines.

While dancing, PRINCE NASTAVIA, PRINCE NICEAVIA, the KING and the QUEEN suddenly appear from nowhere behind PRINCESS PUMPALOT and GUFFY.

F.A.Q stops dancing.

            F.A.Q (CONT'D)
Glad to see my calling dance is working.

            GUFFY
Where did they come from?

PRINCE NASTAVIA, PRINCE NICEAVIA, the KING and the QUEEN look around, wondering how they got there.

            PRINCESS PUMPALOT
    Did you just make them appear from nowhere
    through the medium of dance?

            F.A.Q
    I did. Although not from nowhere. I just
    brought them from wherever they were.

            PRINCE NASTAVIA
Just as well I wasn't sitting on the toilet.

            PRINCE NICEAVIA
Just as well.

The KING stares at F.A.Q.

97

KING

This better be good.

F.A.Q

Your Majesties, Princess and Princes. I have called you here today, as I understand that the Royal Household has a Royal Birthday Ball dilemma.

QUEEN

There's no dilemma. My daughter will go to the Royal Birthday Ball with Prince Nastavia.

PRINCESS PUMPALOT

No, she won't!

QUEEN

Yes, she will!

F.A.Q

Excuse me. I haven't finished yet.

KING

Let the man . . . em, head speak.

F.A.Q

Thank you, Your Majesty. As I was saying before I was so rudely interrupted, the Royal Household has a Royal Birthday Ball dilemma. I have discovered a book, written by Lord Dippy Hughes, in the Royal Archives . . .

PRINCESS PUMPALOT interrupts.

PRINCESS PUMPALOT

Is this the book about the bearded witch and
the flooding?

F.A.Q

Oh no. This is another book. Same author,
different book. This book is called RULES OF
ROYAL BIRTHDAY BALLS WHEN A
FIRST CHILD REACHES 13 ON A
TUESDAY. On page 896, you will see a list
of pre-Ball guidelines. And these guidelines
must be followed to the letter.

KING

But surely we have the final say on any
arrangements?

F.A.Q

You might think that, but for the first child
born on a Tuesday, there are special guidelines.
These guidelines supersede any normal
arrangements made by the King or Queen of
the land.

QUEEN

And if we refuse to follow these guidelines?

There is a BELL sound and a four-inch BEARDED WITCH
appears, floating in mid-air, beside F.A.Q.

The KING recognises the BEARDED WITCH.

KING

It's the Bearded Witch, whose curse meant that
we were sworn to secrecy for 13 years.

QUEEN

Oh, so it is. The photo on the book doesn't do
her justice.

The four-inch BEARDED WITCH begins to speak in a
high-pitched voice.

BEARDED WITCH

Four hundred years ago, I cursed this land
twice. The first curse stated that if the Princess
was ever told about the magic beans before her
13th birthday, the lake would overflow, and the
town of Wiffyville would be washed away.

PRINCESS PUMPALOT

Yes, we know that one.

KING

Can I just confirm that this particular curse
has expired?

BEARDED WITCH

Yes it has.

KING

Jolly good. And the second curse?

The BEARDED WITCH grins.

BEARDED WITCH

The second curse states that if the guidelines
written in the book RULES OF ROYAL
BIRTHDAY BALLS WHEN A FIRST
CHILD REACHES 13 ON A TUESDAY are
not followed, the Queen of the day will turn
into a monkey and the King of the day will
turn into a bottle of maple syrup.

QUEEN

Oh! My goodness! No!

PRINCE NICEAVIA

That is odd.

KING

Maple syrup?

The KING and QUEEN look concerned.

KING (CONT'D)
I really don't think we can go against the guidelines.

QUEEN
Of course not! Bearded Witch, tell us what to do.

The BEARDED WITCH disappears.

QUEEN (CONT'D)
(panicking)
Where's she gone? She didn't tell us what to do!

PRINCESS PUMPALOT turns to the QUEEN.

PRINCESS PUMPALOT
You'd make an excellent monkey.

GUFFY begins to snigger.

QUEEN
This is no laughing matter.

F.A.Q
Don't worry. I know what has to be done.

F.A.Q turns to the KING

F.A.Q (CONT'D)
Your Majesty, can I confirm that you are happy
to follow the guidelines?

KING
I am.

QUEEN

Of course we are!

F.A.Q

And may I have your permission to leave the dungeon to organise the finer points relating to the aforementioned guidelines?

KING

Granted.

F.A.Q

Thank you, Your Majesty.

PRINCESS PUMPALOT

Fak, you still haven't told us what these guidelines are?

F.A.Q

All will be revealed in due course. It's tradition.

PRINCESS PUMPALOT

Not again!

F.A.Q turns to PRINCE NASTAVIA and PRINCE NICEAVIA.

F.A.Q

Prince Nastavia and Prince Niceavia, please step forward.

PRINCE NASTAVIA and PRINCE NICEAVIA move closer to F.A.Q.

F.A.Q (CONT'D)
You must compete to win the Princess's hand
to the Royal Birthday Ball. Be in the Great Hall
tomorrow night at nine o'clock.

CUT TO:

INT. BED CHAMBER - NEXT NIGHT 8:52PM

PRINCESS PUMPALOT is packing her suitcase. GUFFY
walks in.

GUFFY
What are you doing?

PRINCESS PUMPALOT
What does it look like?

GUFFY
You can't just run away.

PRINCESS PUMPALOT
Who said anything about running. I'll take
one of the Royal Bicycles.

GUFFY
Shouldn't you wait to see what the guidelines
reveal?

PRINCESS PUMPALOT
Why? All I know is that there is to be a
competition and the winner will be allowed to

104

PRINCESS PUMPALOT (CONT'D)
take me to the Royal Birthday Ball. There is a
50:50 chance that could be Prince Nastavia. I
should be allowed to choose whom I go to the
Ball with.

There is a loud knock at the door and the sound of a spear
dropping on the floor.

GUFFY
Sidney.

PRINCESS PUMPALOT
Who else?

GUFFY
Looks like it's too late to run.

The door opens and SIDNEY the servant enters.

SIDNEY
Princess Pumpalot. The Queen has asked me
to escort you to the Great Hall.

PRINCESS PUMPALOT
That was very kind of her.

CUT TO:

INT. GREAT HALL - NINE O'CLOCK

The Great Hall is a long narrow hall with oak-panelled walls
and stained glass windows. The walls are covered in heraldic
shields.

SIDNEY the servant and GUFFY stand at the entrance door.

On the other side of the room, the KING, QUEEN and PRINCESS PUMPALOT stand beside each other.

PRINCE NICEAVIA and PRINCE NASTAVIA stand in the middle of the hall facing each other. F.A.Q hovers in mid-air between them.

> F.A.Q
>
> Prince Niceavia and Prince Nastavia. Please make sure you have a gas mask each. Will the Princess please step forward.

PRINCESS PUMPALOT picks up a tin of magic beans from the ground in front of her and stands between PRINCE NICEAVIA and PRINCE NASTAVIA.

> F.A.Q (CONT'D)
>
> Sidney, would you please open the magic beans?

> SIDNEY
>
> Yes, sir.

The QUEEN looks concerned.

Sidney the servant steps forward. He picks up the tin opener and opens the tin of magic beans. He passes the tin to PRINCESS PUMPALOT.

SIDNEY the servant looks pleased with himself. He's finally achieved something without dropping the item or falling over.

106

F.A.Q

Thank you, Sidney.

SIDNEY the servant has a big grin on his face.

F.A.Q (CONT'D)

This is known as a Fart Off. The rules are
as follows. The Princess will eat a green magic
bean which will cause her to release an
extremely potent toxic gas. The Prince who
remains standing the longest will take the
Princess to the Royal Birthday Ball. If the
contest is tied, the Princess can decide with
whom she goes to the Ball. Is that clear?

PRINCE NICEAVIA and PRINCE NASTAVIA nod
in agreement.

PRINCE NASTAVIA

What constitutes a tie?

F.A.Q

A tie will be called if you both remain standing
for exactly the same length of time. The rules
state that you will be timed separately. Can
someone give me a coin to toss?

Prince Niceavia rummages in his pockets and finds a shiny
new coin. He flicks it on to the nose of F.A.Q.

107

PRINCE NICEAVIA
It's one of the new cent coins with Lord Dippy
Hughes on it.

F.A.Q
Very nice it is too. Who wants to call?

PRINCE NASTAVIA
I will. I call heads.

F.A.Q flicks the coin into the air. Much to everyone's
amazement, the coin lands upright on its edge.

F.A.Q
How bizarre. What are the chances of that
happening?

F.A.Q, for a second time, flicks the coin into the air. This time
the coin drops on the floor with the head facing up.

F.A.Q (CONT'D)
Heads it is. Prince Nastavia, would you like to
smell the fart first or second?

PRINCE NASTAVIA
I would like to smell the fart first.

F.A.Q
Okay. Would everyone, apart from Prince
Nastavia, put on their gas mask.

Everyone puts on a gas mask apart from PRINCE
NASTAVIA.

108

PRINCE NASTAVIA
Who will be timing us?

F.A.Q
Geoffrey will be doing the honours.

A small hatch in the ceiling opens. GEOFFREY the giraffe
sticks his head through the hatch. He bows his head towards
the KING and QUEEN. He has a large stopwatch around his
neck.

PRINCE NASTAVIA takes a deep breath.

GEOFFREY
On your marks, get set. Go!

PRINCESS PUMPALOT eats one of the green beans. There is
no noise. It's a silent fart. There is a smell. A very strong smell.

GEOFFREY the giraffe, with his nose, presses the stopwatch
to start.

PRINCE NASTAVIA, after only twelve seconds, collapses on
the floor in a heap.

GEOFFREY the giraffe presses the stopwatch to stop and
opens a window with his head.

Everyone takes their gas mask off.

GEOFFREY (CONT'D)
Twelve seconds.

QUEEN

Only twelve seconds? That's useless.

The KING waves his hand in front of his face. There is a rancid smell in the air.

KING

Mind you, that fart did stink.

QUEEN

Stink? That's an understatement!

KING

I think you can wave goodbye to your ice-cream.

QUEEN

And you can wave goodbye to your cows.

KING

He might still win.

QUEEN

With twelve seconds? You've got to be kidding.

PRINCE NASTAVIA is recovering on the floor. F.A.Q turns to him.

F.A.Q

You best put a gas mask on.

Everyone puts on a gas mask apart from PRINCE NICEAVIA.

PRINCE NICEAVIA takes a deep breath.

GEOFFREY the giraffe closes the window with his head.

> PRINCESS PUMPALOT
> (to Prince Niceavia)
> Come on. You can beat twelve seconds.

> F.A.Q
> Stop that, Princess Pumpalot! You're supposed
> to remain impartial.

> GEOFFREY
> On your marks, get set. Go!

PRINCESS PUMPALOT eats one of the green beans. There is no noise. Just a smell. A very strong smell.

GEOFFREY the giraffe presses the stopwatch to start.

PRINCE NICEAVIA, after only twelve seconds, collapses on the floor in a heap.

GEOFFREY the giraffe presses the stopwatch to stop and opens a window with his head.

Everyone takes their gas mask off.

> GEOFFREY (CONT'D)
> Twelve seconds. It's a tie.

> QUEEN
> I don't believe it.

PRINCE NICEAVIA is still recovering on the floor.

At the entrance door, SIDNEY the servant turns to GUFFY.

> SIDNEY
> (whispering)
> I've just realised why Princess Pumpalot is called Princess Pumpalot.

> GUFFY
> (whispering)
> You're fast.

> SIDNEY
> (whispering)
> It's because she pumps a lot.

> GUFFY
> (whispering)
> Yes, I know!

> SIDNEY
> (whispering)
> That's funny, that is. It means that the King and Queen called her Pumpalot 13 years in advance of her pumping a lot because they knew that . . .

GUFFY interrupts.

> GUFFY
> (whispering louder)
> I know!

PRINCE NICEAVIA gets to his feet.

>   F.A.Q
> This contest has finished in a tie. Princess
> Pumpalot, please step forward and make
> your choice.

The Great Hall falls silent.

PRINCESS PUMPALOT strolls slowly around the Great
Hall in deep thought. She stops walking and stands between
PRINCE NICEAVIA and PRINCE NASTAVIA.

>   PRINCESS PUMPALOT
> I will NOT go to the Royal Birthday Ball with
> Prince Nastavia.

>   QUEEN
> Oh no!

PRINCE NICEAVIA smiles and clenches his fist.

>   PRINCE NICEAVIA
> Yes!

>   PRINCESS PUMPALOT
> And as for Prince Niceavia, I will NOT go to
> the Royal Birthday Ball with him either.

>   QUEEN
> Neither of them?

PRINCESS PUMPALOT looks over to the entrance door.

PRINCESS PUMPALOT

I want to go to the Royal Birthday Ball with
Guffy.

GUFFY looks stunned. He turns to SIDNEY.

GUFFY

What did she say?

SIDNEY

She wants to go to the Royal Birthday Ball
with you.

GUFFY

That's what I thought she said.

The QUEEN faints.

The KING smiles.

PRINCE NASTAVIA, furious, storms out of the Great Hall.

PRINCE NICEAVIA, although disappointed, claps his hands.

CUT TO:

INT. WIFFYVILLE RUGBY CLUB - DAY

The Rugby Club is draped in banners, flowers, rugby shirts
and rugby boots. It's a rugby-themed Royal Birthday Ball.
Even the birthday cake is made in the shape of a rugby ball.

Some of the VILLAGERS have been invited to the Ball. The
guests have been given souvenir gum shields.

PRINCESS PUMPALOT and GUFFY are dancing together in the middle of the floor. They are both wearing rugby shirts, with a number and their name on the back.

The QUEEN turns to the KING.

QUEEN

I can't believe this is happening to me. My only daughter is dancing with a servant at a rugby-themed Royal Birthday Ball. My mother would be turning in her grave.

KING

Just put your gum shield in and look like you're enjoying yourself.

SIDNEY the servant, wearing a smart suit, stands at the back of the room with PRINCE NICEAVIA.

PRINCE NICEAVIA

Day off, Sidney?

SIDNEY

The King gave me time off to attend the Ball.

PRINCE NICEAVIA

That was good of him.

SIDNEY

The Queen wasn't too impressed but she isn't going to change her ways now, is she?

PRINCE NICEAVIA

I suppose not.

SIDNEY

Where's your brother?

PRINCE NICEAVIA

At the police station.

SIDNEY

Why?

PRINCE NICEAVIA

The Police are questioning him about a stolen telescope.

SIDNEY

The one from the observatory?

PRINCE NICEAVIA

The very one.

SIDNEY

Do you think he did it?

PRINCE NICEAVIA

I know he did it.

SIDNEY

I hope you don't mind me saying this. I'm quite glad he's not here today.

PRINCE NICEAVIA

So am I.

SIDNEY

This must be an awkward day for you.

PRINCE NICEAVIA

Why?

SIDNEY

Well, didn't you want to take the Princess to the Ball?

PRINCE NICEAVIA

I did, but as long as the Princess is happy, I'm happy.

SIDNEY
Good for you. You're wise beyond your years.

CUT TO:

EXT. WIFFYVILLE RUGBY CLUB - LATER

GEOFFREY the giraffe is upside down. His legs create a temporary set of rugby posts. PRINCESS PUMPALOT kicks a rugby ball over his legs. Everyone cheers.

Suddenly, four low-flying GNOMES sweep down from the sky and abduct PRINCESS PUMPALOT.

GUFFY
Oh no! The Princess!

PRINCE NICEAVIA
Where did they come from?

It all happened so quickly, no-one was able to do anything.

CUT TO:

INT. KING'S CHAMBERS - LATER

The KING, QUEEN, GUFFY and SIDNEY the servant stare
at the floor. On the floor is a written note beside a rock.

KING
This is a ransom note dropped from the sky. The
low-flying gnomes demand that we surrender
the castle, or the Princess will be tortured.

GUFFY
Tortured? What kind of torture?

KING
I don't know, but it sounds bad.

QUEEN
We need to send out a search party.

KING
Where to?

The QUEEN is panicking.

QUEEN
I don't know where to, but we need to do
something.

PRINCE NICEAVIA stares at the rock.

                    PRINCE NICEAVIA
Wait a minute. I recognise this type of rock.
It's volcanic.

                    QUEEN
This is not the time for a geology lesson.

                    PRINCE NICEAVIA
You're missing the point. There is only one
place near Wiffyville where you'll find volcanic
rock and that's on Jimmy's Hill.

                    QUEEN
Jimmy's Hill?

                    PRINCE NICEAVIA
It's 20 miles south of here, between Emily Hill
and Genny Hill.

                    KING
Brilliant! Well done, Prince Niceavia. We'll
send out a search party tonight.

                    PRINCE NICEAVIA
I'd like to volunteer.

                    KING
No, no, no. This is a royal matter. I'll send
Guffy and Geoffrey.

CUT TO:

EXT. EMILY HILL - NIGHT

It's dark. GEOFFREY the giraffe carries GUFFY on his back. They are wearing night goggles which enable them to see in the dark.

GUFFY has a satchel over his shoulder.

GEOFFREY
Are we nearly there yet?

GUFFY
Every mile you've asked me this. Would you please give it a rest?

GEOFFREY
Sorry. I'm just a little teso.

GUFFY
You're a little what?

GEOFFREY
Teso.

GUFFY
What does that mean?

GEOFFREY
Oh, I forgot to tell you. I'm learning Italian at the moment. Teso means nervous.

121

CUT TO:

INT. PRISON CELL, JIMMY'S HILL - NIGHT

PRINCESS PUMPALOT sits on an old bed in the dark. She touches her neck. The key to the cabinet has gone.

She hears voices in the corridor outside her locked cell door.

PRINCESS PUMPALOT looks through the keyhole and is shocked to see PRINCE NASTAVIA talking to a low-flying GNOME. She gasps. PRINCE NASTAVIA is holding the key to the cabinet.

PRINCESS PUMPALOT sits on the bed and places her face in her hands. She starts to cry.

CUT TO:

EXT. NEAR JIMMY'S HILL - LATER

GEOFFREY the giraffe carries GUFFY on his back. They are getting closer to Jimmy's Hill.

> GEOFFREY
> I was speaking to an old man in the village last week.

> GUFFY
> And?

> GEOFFREY
> He said he knew your great-grandfather.

> GUFFY
> Really.

> GEOFFREY
> He said that your great-grandfather owned a large country house. Is that true?

GUFFY doesn't want to answer.

> GUFFY
> Maybe.

GEOFFREY
The old man said that your great-grandfather
was a Lord. Is that also true?

GUFFY does not really want to talk about this.

GUFFY
Why do you want to know?

GEOFFREY
Just curious.

GUFFY
Well, if you have to know, yes it is true but
don't tell anybody.

GEOFFREY
Why not?

GUFFY sighs.

GUFFY
Titles aren't important. No-one needs to know
this. Can you keep this a secret?

GEOFFREY
My lips are sealed.

CUT TO:

EXT. JIMMY'S HILL - MOMENTS LATER

Jimmy's Hill is now right in front of them.

GEOFFREY

Ecco la Collina di Jimmy.

GUFFY

Let me guess. Translated from Italian, that
means, I can see Jimmy's Hill.

GEOFFREY

Spot on. I'm impressed. You should come to
my Italian class with me on a Tuesday night.

GUFFY

No. It clashes with rugby training.

GEOFFREY

That's a pity.

GUFFY wipes his brow.

GUFFY

The low-flying gnomes have built windows
into the rock.

GEOFFREY

You're right. There are a couple of windows
with bars on them.

GUFFY

Well spotted, Geoffrey.

GEOFFREY

She could be held in one of those.

125

They approach one of the windows and slowly poke their heads up from under the window sill. They cannot believe what they see. PRINCE NASTAVIA is chatting to a low-flying GNOME.

They duck down.

> GUFFY
> Did you see what I saw?

> GEOFFREY
> I hope not.

> GUFFY
> I hope not too.

They once again slowly poke their heads up from under the window sill. Sure enough, PRINCE NASTAVIA is chatting to a low-flying GNOME.

They duck down.

> GUFFY (CONT'D)
> It was him!

> GEOFFREY
> Prince Nastavia!

> GUFFY
> Oh my goodness. What a traitor!

> GEOFFREY
> Shhh! They might hear you.

GEOFFREY the giraffe and GUFFY move over to check another window and slowly poke their heads up from under the window sill. They see PRINCESS PUMPALOT.

GEOFFREY (CONT'D)

There she is.

GUFFY whispers through the bars on the window.

GUFFY

Princess Pumpalot. It's us.

PRINCESS PUMPALOT can't see anything in the darkness. She rushes to the window.

PRINCESS PUMPALOT

Guffy?

GUFFY

Yes. Geoffrey's here too. We're going to rescue you.

PRINCESS PUMPALOT

Do you know that Prince Nastavia is here?

GUFFY

Yes. We saw him.

PRINCESS PUMPALOT

He's working with the low-flying gnomes!

GUFFY

Unbelievable!

PRINCESS PUMPALOT
If I ever get my hands on him I'll . . .

GEOFFREY the giraffe interrupts PRINCESS PUMPALOT.

GEOFFREY
Your Royal Highness, there will be time for all
that later. Our present concern is getting you
out. Are there any bed sheets on your bed?

PRINCESS PUMPALOT
Why?

GEOFFREY
If I can tie one side of a bed sheet to the bars
and the other side to my legs, I can probably
pull the bars off.

PRINCESS PUMPALOT
There are no sheets on the bed. It's a duvet.

GUFFY
I don't think that will work.

GEOFFREY
Any rope in your room?

PRINCESS PUMPALOT
No.

GEOFFREY
Is there anything in your room we can use?

PRINCESS PUMPALOT

There's a cup and a teaspoon.

GUFFY

I don't think that will work.

GUFFY taps GEOFFREY the giraffe on his head.

GUFFY (CONT'D)

Geoffrey, why don't you just head butt the bars?

GEOFFREY

What? That'll be really sore!

GUFFY

It's the Princess we're talking about here.
Come on.

GEOFFREY the giraffe thinks for a second or two. He looks at GUFFY and then PRINCESS PUMPALOT.

GEOFFREY

Okay. You're right. Stand away from the bars,
your Royal Highness.

PRINCESS PUMPALOT

Hold on. The guards on the other side of the
door might hear you. If only I had a tin of
magic beans, I could knock them out with a
green one.

GUFFY reaches into his satchel. He pulls out a tin of magic
beans and a tin opener. He opens the tin and hands it to
PRINCESS PUMPALOT.

GUFFY
I had a funny feeling you might need these.

PRINCESS PUMPALOT
You're a star.

PRINCESS PUMPALOT eats one of the green beans. There is no noise. Just a smell. A very strong smell.

There is a thudding noise from behind the cell door.

PRINCESS PUMPALOT (CONT'D)
I believe that was the sound of two guards collapsing in the corridor outside my cell door. Right, I'm ready to go.

GEOFFREY
Your Royal Highness, move away from the window, please.

GEOFFREY the giraffe head butts the bars. The bars move slightly apart.

He head butts the bars again. This time the bars move a sufficient distance to create a space for PRINCESS PUMPALOT to escape.

GEOFFREY the giraffe is now dizzy.

PRINCESS PUMPALOT squeezes between the bars and jumps on GEOFFREY the giraffe's back. She grabs hold of GUFFY around the waist.

GEOFFREY the giraffe tries to run but stumbles. This alerts

the low-flying GNOMES.

PRINCE NASTAVIA looks out of a window but can't see anything in the dark.

GEOFFREY the giraffe picks himself up and moves quickly away from Jimmy's Hill.

The low-flying GNOMES can't see in the dark either. They fire a number of arrows more in hope than expectation. The arrows miss GEOFFREY the giraffe, PRINCESS PUMPALOT and GUFFY.

> PRINCESS PUMPALOT
> The key! The key! They have the key to the cabinet.

> GUFFY
> We can't go back.

> PRINCESS PUMPALOT
> We'll have to. We can't leave the key behind.

> GUFFY
> You're not thinking straight. If they've got the key, let them come to us.

> PRINCESS PUMPALOT
> I don't understand.

> GUFFY
> The key is only useful to them if they have the magic beans too. So let's wait for them to come to us!

131

CUT TO:

EXT. WIFFYVILLE PARK, BESIDE THE LAKE - DAY

GEOFFREY the giraffe and SIDNEY the servant sit on a bench eating lunch.

                    SIDNEY
        How's your head?

                    GEOFFREY
        Better, thanks.

                    SIDNEY
        You were very brave going to Jimmy's Hill.

                    GEOFFREY
        I'm sure you'd have done the same if asked.

                    SIDNEY
        Probably.

                    GEOFFREY
        Did you hear about Guffy?

                    SIDNEY
        No. What about Guffy?

GEOFFREY pauses for a second.

                    GEOFFREY
        I can't say. I'm sworn to secrecy.

                    SIDNEY
        I can keep a secret.

                         GEOFFREY
          Well don't tell anybody.

                          SIDNEY
          I promise not to.

GEOFFREY looks over his shoulder, checking no-one is
around.

                         GEOFFREY
                    (whispering)
          Guffy's great-grandfather was a Lord.

SIDNEY is surprised.

                          SIDNEY
          A log?

                         GEOFFREY
          No. A Lord.

                          SIDNEY
          Good Lord!

                                              CUT TO:

INT. LORD DIPPY HUGHES'S LIBRARY - DAY

LORD DIPPY HUGHES is watering his cactus plant.

                    LORD DIPPY HUGHES
          A word of advice. Never ask anybody to keep a
          secret, as this invariably leads to them telling
          someone else. On this occasion, Sidney told

                            133

LORD DIPPY HUGHES (CONT'D)
Loots. Loots told Prince Niceavia and Prince
Niceavia told the King.

LORD DIPPY HUGHES smiles.

LORD DIPPY HUGHES (CONT'D)
You should have seen the Queen's face when
she found out.

CUT TO:

INT. CASTLE DUNGEONS - LATER

PRINCESS PUMPALOT and GUFFY are in front of the
cabinet. F.A.Q is floating in mid-air.

F.A.Q
The low-flying gnomes might surprise us.

PRINCESS PUMPALOT
They won't get anywhere near us. The trap is set.

F.A.Q
Why is Geoffrey not here to help?

GUFFY
He's too big to fit in the dungeon.

F.A.Q
And Sidney?

GUFFY
He's guarding the King and Queen.

F.A.Q

Are you sure the net will fall on them when
they walk past the purple wheelbarrow?

GUFFY

We've tried it a dozen times. It works a treat.
They have to come this way to get to the
cabinet. It's all set. Nothing can go wrong.

F.A.Q

Don't say that. You're tempting fate.

GUFFY

Look, calm down. The Princess has an open tin
of magic beans lined up just in case there's a
problem, but there won't be.

PRINCESS PUMPALOT, GUFFY and F.A.Q sit quietly for
half an hour. Nothing happens. They all fall asleep.

CUT TO:

EXT. WIFFYVILLE VILLAGE - EVENING

PRINCE NASTAVIA walks briskly through the village.

We see an aerial view of the guardhouse. LOOTS'S tennis
rackets have by pure chance created an X shape on the
guardhouse roof. Six low-flying GNOMES use the roof as a
landing point.

PRINCE NASTAVIA reaches the entrance to the castle
tunnel. He is followed by the six low-flying GNOMES.

135

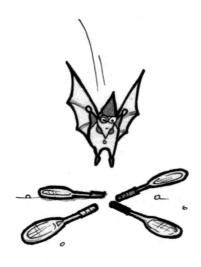

LOOTS moves forward with a tennis racket in his right hand.

LOOTS
Who goes there?

PRINCE NASTAVIA
Prince Nastavia.

LOOTS
What is your business in the castle?

PRINCE NASTAVIA
I have an appointment with Princess Pumpalot.

LOOTS notices the six low-flying GNOMES.

LOOTS
Wait a minute! Are they low-flying gnomes?

PRINCE NASTAVIA
No.

                              LOOTS
Okay. On you go, then.

                        PRINCE NASTAVIA
                        (under his breath)
Unbelievable!

                                                    CUT TO:

INT. CASTLE DUNGEONS - MOMENTS LATER

PRINCE NASTAVIA, carrying a map, walks through the
castle tunnel. He is followed by six low-flying GNOMES.
He walks past the purple wheelbarrow but the net doesn't fall
on him.

He appears from the dark dungeon and stands in front of
PRINCESS PUMPALOT, GUFFY and F.A.Q who are still
asleep.

                        PRINCE NASTAVIA
                Well, well, well. What do we have here?

PRINCESS PUMPALOT, GUFFY and F.A.Q wake from
their sleep. The low-flying GNOMES grab hold of them.

                    PRINCE NASTAVIA (CONT'D)
            Is this the last line of defence? Honestly, you
            are all so pathetic. I have the key to the cabinet.
            The magic beans will mean I can take over the
            whole of Wiffyville and invade many other lands.

PRINCESS PUMPALOT
You really are a horror.

PRINCE NASTAVIA
Well, thank you. I'll take that as a compliment. Right, move aside and let me get the key into the cabinet door.

F.A.Q can't help but move into automatic mode. He wriggles free from his captors and floats in mid-air.

F.A.Q
You must ask at least five of the top ten frequently asked questions before venturing further.

PRINCE NASTAVIA
Get out the way, you body-less freak! I'm not going to ask any stupid questions.

PRINCE NASTAVIA pushes F.A.Q out of the way and approaches the cabinet.

Then, from the darkness, PRINCE NICEAVIA appears behind PRINCE NASTAVIA.

PRINCE NICEAVIA
Stop right there!

PRINCE NASTAVIA turns.

PRINCE NASTAVIA
Ha! It's the wimp. What are you going to do?

PRINCE NICEAVIA

I'm going to do what I should have done a
long time ago.

PRINCE NASTAVIA

And what is that?

PRINCE NICEAVIA

I'm going to . . .

Before he can finish his sentence, PRINCE NICEAVIA
passes the purple wheelbarrow and a net falls on his head.
He struggles in the net but he can't escape.

PRINCE NICEAVIA (CONT'D)
I'm not finished with you.

PRINCE NASTAVIA laughs.

PRINCE NASTAVIA
You're such a loser.

F.A.Q
That's tragic.

PRINCESS PUMPALOT
At least he tried.

GUFFY
I told you the net would work.

PRINCE NASTAVIA
All of you, shut up!

PRINCE NASTAVIA takes out the key to the cabinet and moves closer to the cabinet.

PRINCE NASTAVIA pushes the key into the cabinet lock. He slowly turns the key. There's a puff of smoke and whoosh, PRINCE NASTAVIA turns into a mouse.

The six low-flying GNOMES jump up in shock, releasing PRINCESS PUMPALOT in the process.

PRINCESS PUMPALOT quickly reaches for the open tin of magic beans. She eats one of the red beans and bends over. There is a gurgling noise and Phhhhhhhart - the six low-flying GNOMES are flattened against the dungeon wall.

140

PRINCESS PUMPALOT

Take that!

CUT TO:

INT. KING'S CHAMBERS - LATER

The KING, QUEEN, PRINCESS PUMPALOT and GUFFY are celebrating with an ice-cream from the famous Antonio triplets of Wiffyville.

QUEEN
Chocolate sorbet. Yum. Yum.

The KING leans over the table to speak to PRINCESS PUMPALOT.

KING
We are so happy you're safe.

PRINCESS PUMPALOT
Thank you, father.

QUEEN
I confess, I was wrong about Prince Nastavia.

PRINCESS PUMPALOT
It's really shocking.

QUEEN
Really, really shocking! And I was wrong about Guffy too.

PRINCESS PUMPALOT
Guffy too?

                    QUEEN
        Did you not hear? Guffy's great-grandfather was
        a Lord.

GUFFY shakes his head. GEOFFREY the giraffe has clearly
not kept his secret.

              PRINCESS PUMPALOT
        What difference does that make?

                    QUEEN
        A big difference. He's from good stock.

              PRINCESS PUMPALOT
        Don't be silly.

                    QUEEN
        Don't call me silly.

The KING steps between them.

                    KING
        Will you just stop it! This is meant to be a
        happy day.

A small hatch in the ceiling opens. GEOFFREY the giraffe
sticks his head through the hatch. He bows his head towards
the KING and the QUEEN.

                  GEOFFREY
        Sua Maesta'. Sono stato appena informato del
        fatto che il Principe Nastavia dovra' presentarsi
        in corte il prossimo lunedi'.

There is an awkward silence.

                    GUFFY
          It's in Italian.

                    KING
          I gathered that much.

                    QUEEN
          Can we have a translation?

The KING attempts to translate.

                    KING
          Principe Nastavia must mean Prince Nastavia.
          Lunedi is Monday. Corte probably means . . .

The QUEEN interrupts.

                    QUEEN
          Not you! I want Geoffrey to translate.

GEOFFREY the giraffe bows his head.

                    GEOFFREY
          Your Majesties, I have just been informed that
          Prince Nastavia will appear in court on Monday.

The QUEEN claps her hands.

                    QUEEN
          Excellent news.

KING

I was about to say corte probably means court.

There is a gurgling noise emanating from PRINCESS
PUMPALOT'S tummy.

KING (CONT'D)

Is that what I think it is?

QUEEN

I think it might be.

The QUEEN takes cover under her throne. The KING hides
under the table. GUFFY hides behind a chair.

PRINCESS PUMPALOT farts. Nothing happens.

PRINCESS PUMPALOT

It's okay. It's just a normal fart.

The KING and QUEEN begin to laugh. PRINCESS
PUMPALOT and GUFFY join in.

PRINCESS PUMPALOT then sneezes, farts and hiccups at
the same time.

PRINCESS PUMPALOT (CONT'D)

And that's known as a 'snartup'!

Laughter can be heard echoing around the castle.

CUT TO:

INT. LORD DIPPY HUGHES'S LIBRARY - DAY

LORD DIPPY HUGHES is standing beside a bookshelf. He has a large dusty book open in front of him.

> LORD DIPPY HUGHES
> Prince Nastavia appeared in Wiffyville County Court. Several mouse traps were set around the courtroom to prevent him from escaping. He was found guilty of treason (and stealing the Village Observatory's telescope). As a punishment he was sent to Wiffyville prison (with the six low-flying gnomes) for three years. His bungalows in the village were confiscated and demolished and the old cottages were re-built on the site to once again form a smiley face.

LORD DIPPY HUGHES closes the book and places it on the bookshelf.

> LORD DIPPY HUGHES (CONT'D)
> And as for Princess Pumpalot and Guffy? That's another story.

We see the title of the book on the spine: PRINCESS PUMPALOT (THE FARTING PRINCESS).

This is what the Queen would have looked
like if she'd been turned into a monkey.